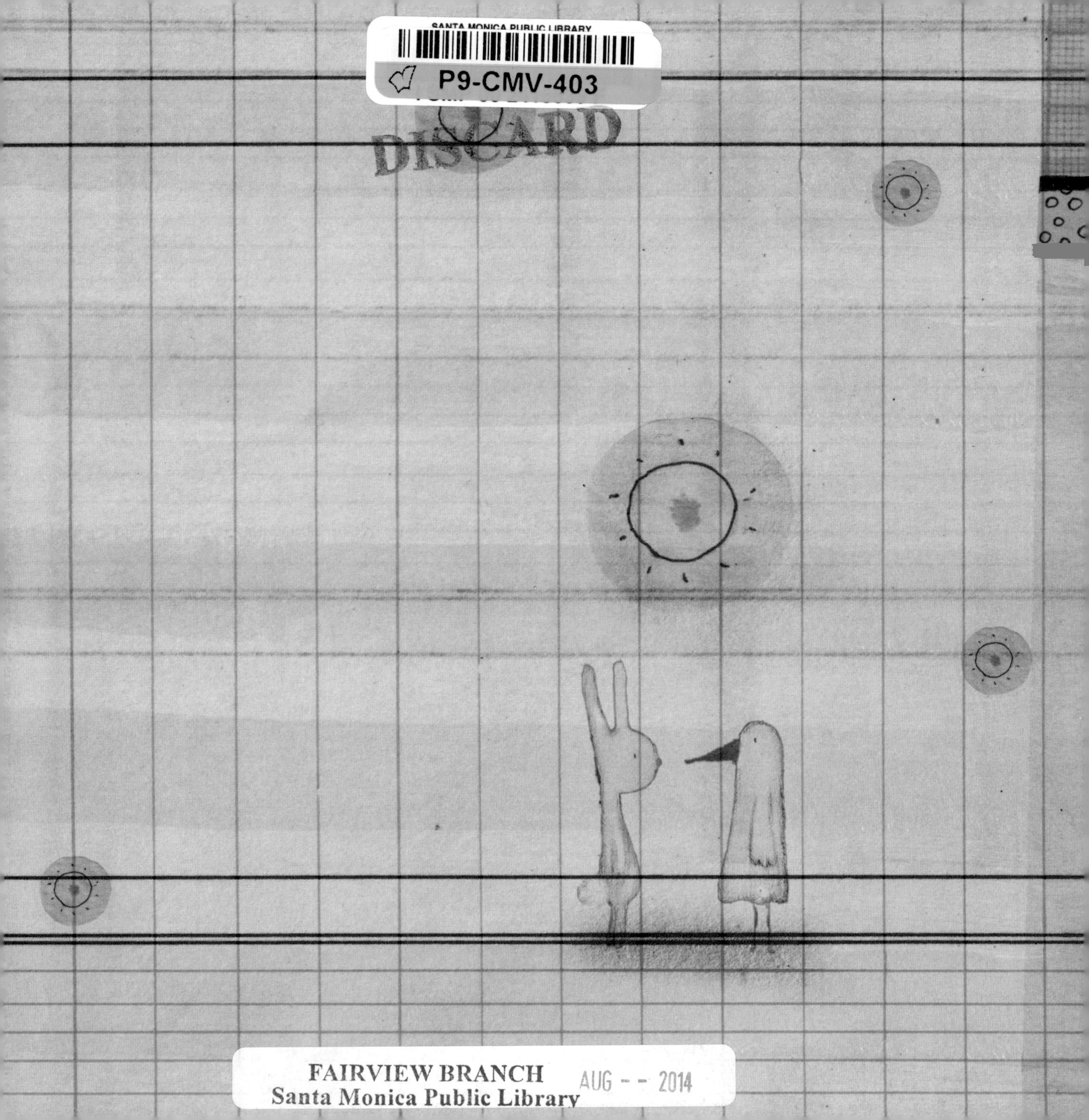

Obra ganadora del «I Premio Internacional Compostela para álbumes ilustrados».

El jurado estuvo formado por:
Miguel Calatayud, Xabier P. Docampo, Fernando Krahn, Guadalupe Rodríguez,
Manuela Rodríguez, Xosé M. Rodríguez-Abella, Marc Taeger, Beatriz Varela y Óscar Villán.

Avión Cuatro Vientos, 7
41013 Sevilla
Telefax: 954 095 558
andalucia@kalandraka.com
www.kalandraka.com

Impreso en C/A Gráfica, Vigo
Primera edición: octubre, 2008
ISBN: 978-84-96388-88-8
DL: SE 4128-2008

NATALIA COLOMBO

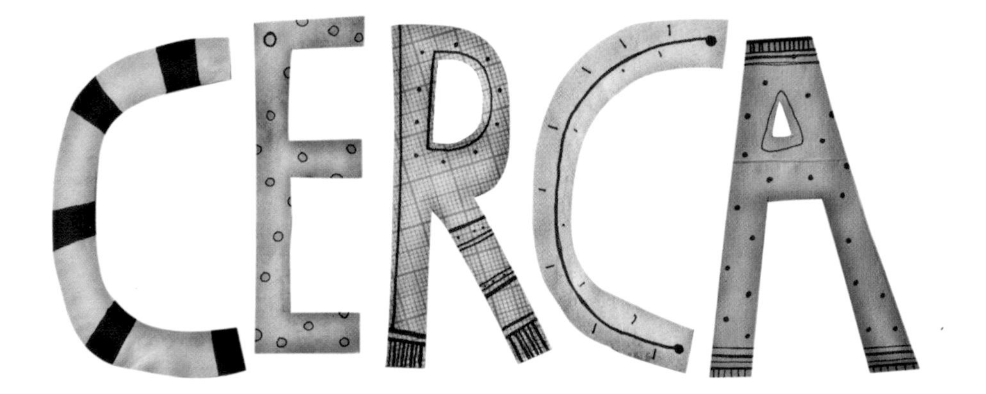

kalandraka

EL SEÑOR PATO,
COMO TODOS LOS DÍAS,
SE VA A TRABAJAR.

El señor conejo,
como todos los días,
también se va
a trabajar.

Siempre se cruzan.

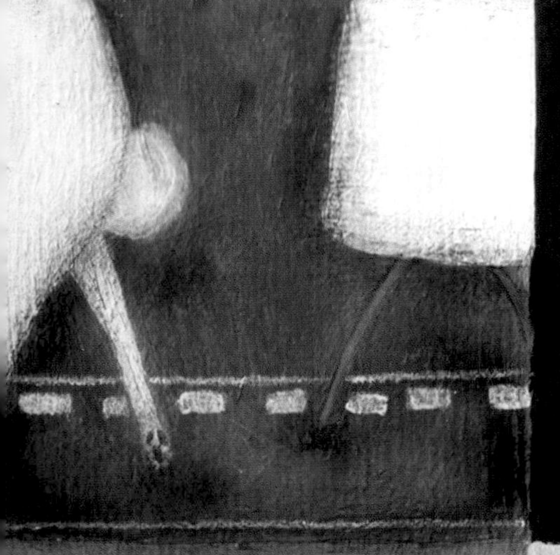

CUANDO
VAN...

Y CUANDO
VIENEN.

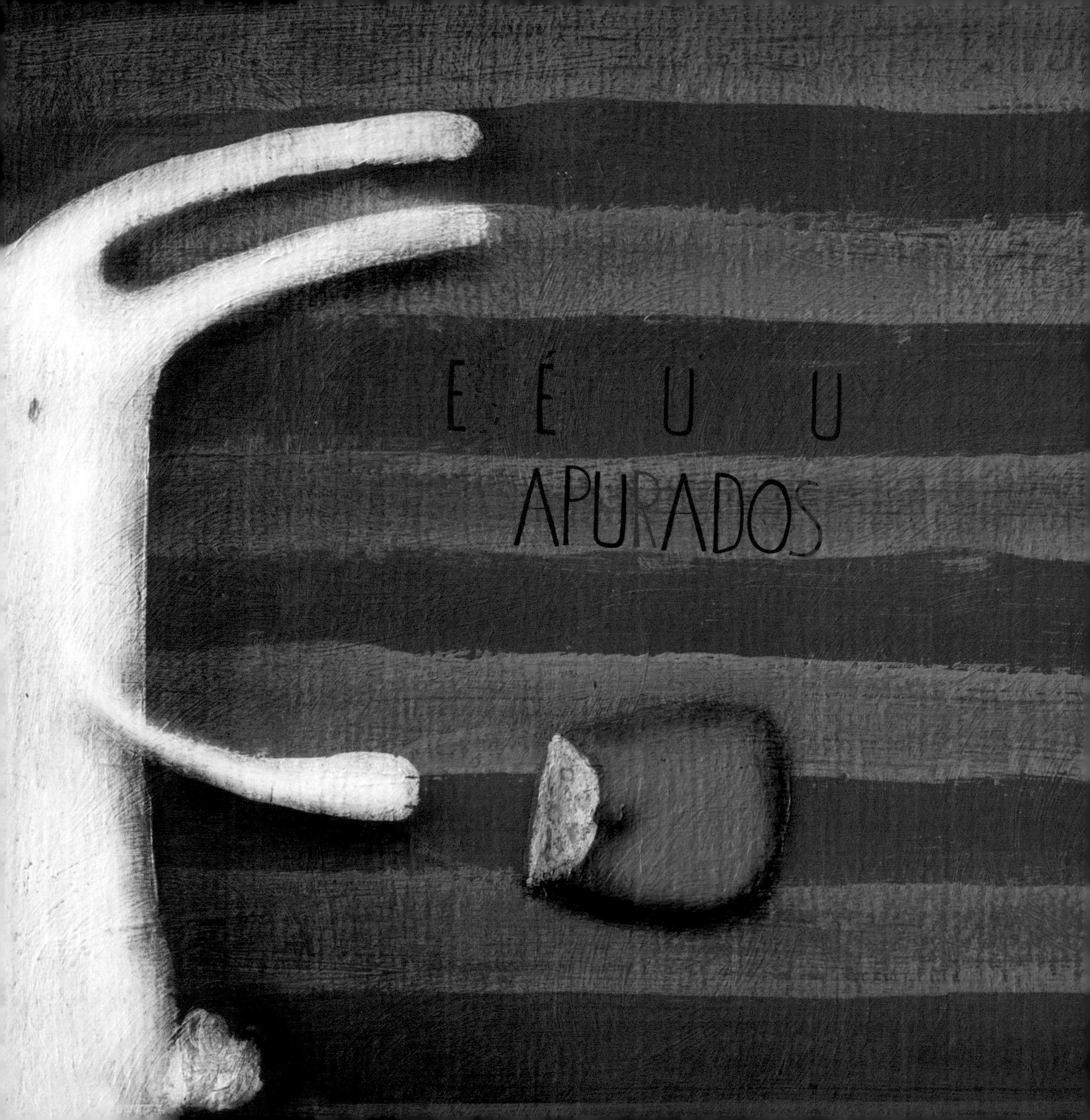
E É U U
APURADOS

NO

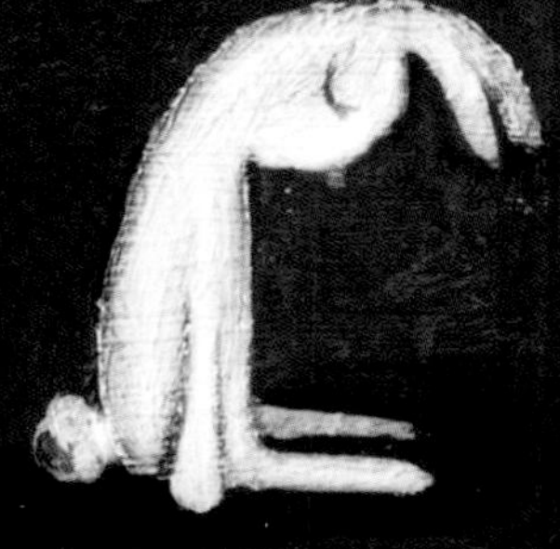

O NO...

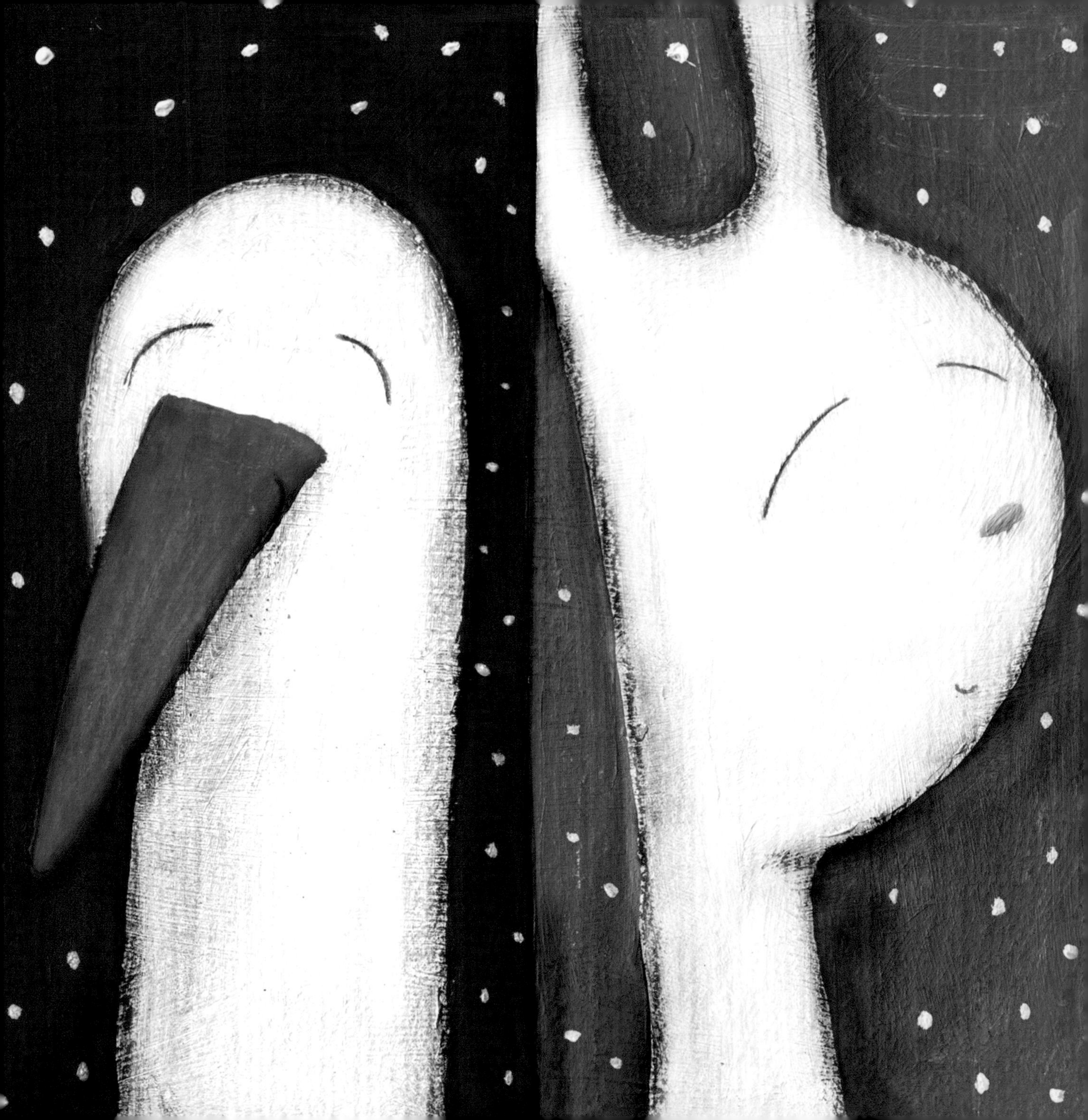

EN LA PLAZA...

CUANDO VIAJAN...

EN EL PARQUE...

NUNCA SE SALUDAN.

Y ES
UNA VERDADERA

PENA...

PODRÍAN SER GRANDES AMIGOS.

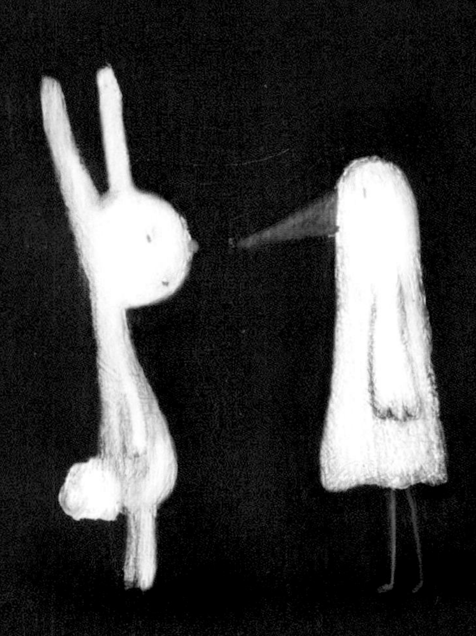

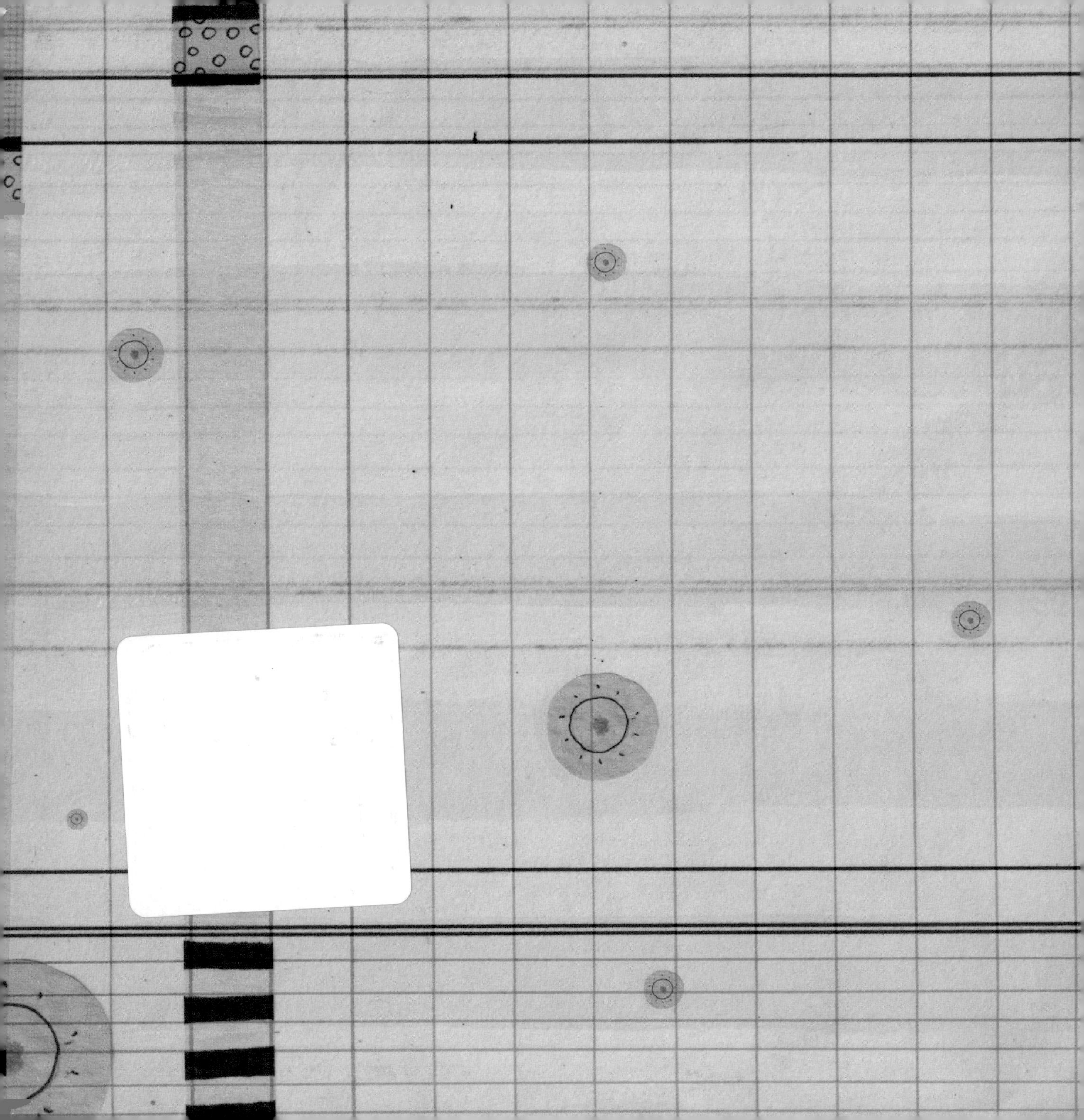

P9-AZV-058

Little Ghoul Goes to School

Jef Czekaj

SUNSHINE ELEMENTARY

BALZER & BRAY
An Imprint of HarperCollins*Publishers*

 • For information address HarperCollins Children's Books, a division of HarperCollins Publishers, 195 Broadway, New York, NY 10007. • www.harpercollinschildrens.com • ISBN 978-0-06-244111-9 • The artist used ink on paper and digitally colored in Adobe Photoshop to create the illustrations for this book. • Typography by Chelsea C. Donaldson • 21 22 23 24 25 RTLO 10 9 8 7 6 5 4 3 2 1 ❖ First Edition

To Veta and Ollie

Tomorrow was the first day of school, and Little Ghoul was nervous.

"Don't worry, my little maggot," said her mother. "I'm sure school will be just ghastly!"

Her mom sat with her and explained how horrible the first day of school would be.

It made Little Ghoul feel a little better.

Little Ghoul devoured a bedtime snack.

She brushed her teeth with rotten-onion-flavored toothpaste.

She jumped into bed. Her mom slobbered on her and tenderly said, "I hope you have dreadful nightmares."

Z
Z
Z

Little Ghoul was still thinking about school as she closed her eyes and drifted off to sleep.

When Little Ghoul's eyes popped open, it was morning.

She had been hoping the weather for her first day of school would be her favorite: cold and rainy.

But, alas, it was bright and sunny.

Her mom licked her goodbye, and Little Ghoul headed to the bus stop.

Her mom had explained that the school bus would be an old scrap heap with a terrifying driver.

But when it arrived, the bus looked safe, and the driver was friendly.

"Welcome aboard!" he said.

This was awful. But that wasn't nearly as bad as when they arrived at school.

The principal waited outside to greet everyone with a huge smile on her face.

"Good morning! It's great to see you!" Principal Edelman said.

Little Ghoul hoped the classroom would be dark and dank and the teacher would be mean.

But she was disappointed again.

At least lunch would be disgusting. . . .

Her mom had promised to pack her favorite:

a maggot-and-brown-banana-peel sandwich, rotten milk, and a pickle-and-fishbone cookie for dessert.

But inside her lunch box she found a peanut-butter-and-jelly sandwich. There was even a chocolate chip cookie!

Ewwwwww!

At this point, Little Ghoul was sure that she hated school.

She sat on the floor as the librarian explained how they would use their library cards.

There was something familiar about Ms. Shelley, but Little Ghoul couldn't quite put her finger on it.

Ms. Shelley told them that each student would get to take a library book home.

Little Ghoul had a hard time choosing.

Luckily, Ms. Shelley had a suggestion.

Then it was time for art class.

Little Ghoul made a mess. She tore paper. She threw paint. She glued scraps of fabric to the torn paper and thrown paint.

"Wow," said Mr. Ryder, the art teacher. "That's powerful. I can really feel the energy and emotion in your work. Let's put it in the student art show!"

Just when Little Ghoul was thinking she might actually survive the first day of school, the unthinkable happened.

"Hi," said a smiling boy. "My name is Ben. Let's be friends!"

Friends? *Friends?* Ghouls don't have friends! Ghouls are too creepy, spooky, and spine-chilling to have friends!

So Little Ghoul did the only sensible thing she could think of.

She ran away, screaming.

Little Ghoul was still screaming
when she opened her eyes.

"Mom, I dreamed that I went to
school and everyone was nice!
It was awful."

"Oh, my little maggot," said her mom, "that was just a dream. Now it's time for you to get ready for your *real* first day of school."

Little Ghoul was nervous as she headed to the bus stop.

But happily, the weather was cold and rainy.

The school bus was rusty and filled with unsavory creatures.

Her teacher was hideous.

Lunch was absolutely repulsive.

And when she saw the librarian, Ms. Shelley . . .

Little Ghoul knew everything would be all right.